T0198834

Tourette's and Me

Written By Zechariah D. Watts

Illustrated by Jane Luna

To order additional copies of this book, contact:
Xlibris
844-714-8691
www.Xlibris.com
Orders@Xlibris.com

ISBN: Softcover   979-8-3694-0124-8
         EBook   979-8-3694-0123-1

Print information available on the last page

Rev. date: 06/24/2023

THIS BOOK IS FOR ANYONE WITH TIC DISORDER AND TOURETTES SYNDROME.

I WISH I COULD SIT QUIETLY

BUT MY SHOULDERS KEEP JUMPING

UP AND DOWN!

I WISH I COULD FOCUS MY EYES

AND READ BUT THEY JUST

KEEP BLINKING!

I WISH I DIDN'T MAKE FUNNY NOISES

BUT I CAN'T HELP IT!

SOMETIMES PEOPLE STARE AT ME
AND SOMETIMES THEY LAUGH

SO WHY NOT MAKE SOME
HUMOR OUT OF IT.

IT'S BEDTIME BUT I'M STILL GROOVING AND DANCING TO MY TOURETTE SYNDROME.

BECAUSE THIS IS THE LIFE

WITH TOURETTE'S AND ME!

Printed in the United States
by Baker & Taylor Publisher Services